TOMORROW'S PROMISE

IMOGENE NIX

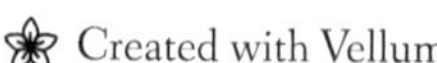 Created with Vellum

For my FamilyIt's strange writing a new dedication for the print version but on the other hand its also exciting, given this title has never been in print.
But as always, the first people I must thank are my tribe - Sassie, Keri and Suzi. Without you wonderful ladies, I wouldn't be anywhere near this today.
Thanks also to my family. You know why.
Lastly, thanks to the wonderful readers who have believed in me all the way along and keep buying my books!

Imogene
2019

CHAPTER 1

David stood still—frozen— the sound of crunching gravel filling the air behind him under the warm midday sun. Emma Rose had loved this section of the park, with the swings and slides, until she had been too ill to visit anymore.

"Daddy, swing me higher!" He could still hear her voice echoing in his mind. "Oh, Daddy, I love the park!"

His heart was a heavy brick as the memories of her short life swirled in his mind.

The loss of Emma Rose had killed the dwindling fire between him and Karin; and after her passing, they'd agreed their futures did not include each other as lovers.

"We just didn't fit anymore," he murmured.

Memories of their bitter arguments pulsed.

"*I need your help...*" and "*I can't do this on my own...*"

His memory of Karin's words burned in his chest.

Of his many failures.

Their tenuous connection broken, they went their separate ways, neither able to cope with the pressures and stresses that came with the loss of a child.

David watched the stems of purple flowers waving in the slight breeze contrasting with the gauzy fabrics of those gathered around. The collar at his neck itched, and he tugged, no longer used to the constriction of a tie.

Music swelled around him, and laughter filled the air.

Pain radiated through his soul.

Emma Rose would've been seven today.

"If only you were here," he muttered, the all-too-familiar ache in his chest. Every day, but especially on *this* anniversary, there was that hole in his heart, and he'd find any way to fill it up.

He didn't want to forget her. Never that. Just, maybe make the ache go away.

"David? I know this is hard for you, but she's happy." A hand clasped his shoulder. Karin's brother, Gordon implored him.

He nodded, seeing Martine, Gordon's wife standing behind him.

Of course, they didn't fully appreciate his state of melancholy, today of all days.

They'd both watched the grief cloud his ability to think, then swallow him. David had allowed it to push her—Karin — away from him.

They thought it was all about the loss of the relationship. That she'd moved on and found another love.

He didn't intend to explain, because the pain was personal and in a strange way, intimate.

"I know."

Only Michael knew the full truth of the depth of the despair he'd felt at the death of Emma Rose.

"Yeah. We're still here for you, though." Another voice, and a softer hand this time held his.

Martine.

Gordon's wife had been a staunch supporter during the troubled months that'd passed. She'd helped him claw out of the misery when he'd finally reached rock bottom of the alcoholic fugue.

They were the reason he was still here.

He gripped her hand, seeking that support again.

Echoes of people laughing and celebrating floated over him. A bandstand sat in the middle of the fragrant gardens, decked out in ribbons and balloons of muted pastels, proclaiming today to be a life-affirming celebration. Groups of people held champagne glasses and toasted another rite of passage.

A wedding.

A soft wind blew, rather like a kiss against his cheek, and he raised a hand, savoring the connection. For a moment, he allowed the whimsical notion Emma Rose was there, consoling him, warming his chilled body until a trick of heat released the frozen sensation in his fingers.

Memories of his daughter smiling bathed him in a sense of peace.

The sound level rose, swelling as the band played the traditional march and the bride moved forward.

The red carpet was a foil for her pale pink ankle length gown, and she beamed, the hand resting on her gravid belly preceding her. Declaring that life went on.

Karin.

Today she was marrying his friend, Michael.

His best friend.

Truly, he was happy for her. For them both.

Someone jostled him from behind, but he ignored it, focusing on the tableau in front of him.

"Sorry."

He heard the word but kept his gaze in front.

I feel like an interloper.

David needed to stay, watch, as they became man and wife, celebrating with their combined friends. He'd support Karin today, guessing it was probably a high *and* low point for her.

Sadness warred with burgeoning hope and he shifted his feet. "Damned shoes." He focused on his discomfort, hoping to subdue the boiling emotions.

Even at this distance, he detected a hint of sadness in her eyes, the way she clutched the small lilies close, the trembling way she wiped a tear from her face.

He shuddered, refusing to release a moan as the echoes of the past nearly overtook him again, tearing and clawing from the inside, as if some ravening beast needing to escape.

How he wished Emma Rose was here to join them in this celebration. She would've loved the gowns, the music and the way the laughter filled the air.

He sighed again. Needed to pull out of his funk before it consumed him. His life needed to move on too.

David caught sight of a woman, some distance away.

Her face was set, as if she too was pained by this event.

She wasn't classically beautiful. The shape of her jaw sharply etched, all lines and angles, her stunning eyes far too piercing to be anything other than striking.

"Who's the woman over there?" he asked Gordon.

"I don't know." His former brother-in-law was distracted, watching the exchange of rings.

David could tell she wasn't comfortable in the gown she wore, either. Her awkwardness was clear in the way she shifted and moved, as if it scratched or slumped.

Her fingers kept adjusting the bodice so it covered her

chest. The well-toned look of her demanded he look and keep looking at her—not the bride.

Mesmerized, he studied her face.

The play of emotions, pain, and loss joined with anger and a hint of something a little darker. She tried to conceal it with her careful smiles—the same way he did—but he could see it in her stance.

In many ways, she also reminded him of Emma Rose, who'd tried to hide her pain and fear at the end. He cut the thought off, determined to focus on the celebrations in front of him.

For the first time in a long time, sexual interest and something else far too precious to name, sparked deep inside David.

Genie wanted to scream.

Blind Freddy could see Michael loved her and she loved him.

"Will you keep this promise?" The words echoed through the tiny pavilion, and she'd have an aching face from the smile she plastered on.

Her heart rebelled.

She and Michael had been in the same platoon for years, accepting whatever postings came their way.

They'd always ended up together. The way they'd been mucking in on so many missions had forged a fast friendship over the years. A connection she'd stupidly believed was a sign they belonged together.

"Will you honor the memories you are making together?"

The ceremony continued as she tugged once more at the bodice. She could swear it was about to fail.

And wouldn't that be the ultimate insult? Bridesmaid loses dress at the wedding of the man she lusts over! Urgh!

Michael rarely talked of anyone, except Karin. How strong she was. How graceful.

That'd burned her butt the whole time, but she'd smiled and listened.

Karin had apparently been married before, to a guy named David, which made her unattainable for Michael. He'd told her so countless times.

Or that was what they'd all thought until Karin and David had separated. Stupidly, Genie had always thought there was time to prove how they belonged together.

"I will."

Too late!

She'd always been far too late.

Genie controlled the burning tears.

Michael repeated their vows, his voice clear and loud, and she had an overwhelming desire to gallop to the front, to tell them they were making a mistake.

She locked her knees instead, and gripped the anguish within her tighter, using it as a barrier against the pain.

"Hey Genie! Guess what? Karin and David broke up. I know it's soon, but I'm going to be there for her. I've loved her for so long, but they were married. Now they're not. I don't want to disrespect David, because he's my friend but..." He'd smiled at her, as if willing her to understand.

To Michael, Karin was the perfect woman. The one Genie had hoped would falter so she could take her place beside him. It would've been Genie and Mike. But no more.

The dream is shattered.

The bottom had dropped out of her world. *"I'm... I'm pleased for you Mike."*

He'd clapped her on the back and passed a beer. "She's raw. What with Emma Rose's death. I know it's been six months, but she's battling and felt so lonely. Genie? How do I help her?"

She'd looked at him. *"I don't know, Mike. I've never had a husband or child or lost either. I guess be yourself?"* The words had sounded lame, but there wasn't much else she could do.

Genie banished the memory. Today wasn't the time or place for wallowing publicly.

The ring slipped onto the bride's finger, and it was done.

They were married, and Michael was beyond her reach now.

Here I am... A bridesmaid at their wedding. Supposedly helping them celebrate their future together.

The truth ate at her like acid, but the essential part of her refused to allow her to ruin it for them. For him.

Karin had asked her as Michael's friend, and damn it, how could she possibly say no?

The couple had even chosen Emma Rose's birthday for their wedding day, hoping in some small way to remember her in the ceremony, all the while flaunting the belly full of baby which made Michael ecstatically happy.

His eyes glinted with a light she'd never seen

"Don't they look happy?" The girl standing beside her chattered, and Genie nodded.

They did.

She had to deal with the huge oily waves of jealousy she couldn't control roiling within her stomach.

"It's great that they chose Emma Rose's birthday.

Making sure she isn't forgotten." The young woman prattled on while the bride and groom signed the paperwork with an elaborate feather pen.

Although, Genie tried to tune her words out, she couldn't.

"She would've been seven today. She was so cute and sweet." Her choked voice trailed away as she wiped at a tear with a tissue.

Genie tugged on the form fitting light pink gown of satin and tulle. Only for Michael would she endure this color and style. Shame he'd never know that though, her mind slyly reminded her.

It was too late now.

That little baby inside the bride told her there was no future in weaving impossible dreams.

Finally the ceremony came to an end.

"Look!" the crowd ebbed, as she too watched as the release of snowy white doves. Everyone *oohed* and *ahhed*.

She experienced a sharper bite of jealousy, one she covered up with tight smiles and nods.

The back of her neck prickled and itched as she joined the recessional, gliding up the red carpet, and she fought the urge to turn and see what or who was causing it.

A small restaurant lay ahead, and she gave a silent sigh of relief. *'What a beautiful bride,'* and *'We couldn't be happier for them,'* echoed around as she plodded forward and up to the small white building, feet stinging in the flimsy heels as the rocks crunched underfoot.

Her silly heel caught on a board as she rose up the steps, and a firm hand gripped her arm. "I have you."

Warmth spread through her from the point of contact, and the liquid voice made her knees wobble with the intention of melting. "Thanks."

The hand stayed, and she wanted to move closer toward it, because the trickle of electricity was so inviting. Her breathing shallowed out, and she shivered.

"You're cold?"

That voice again, and this time she turned.

Her eyes took in the tanned face, deeply lined, showing the trials and tribulations of his life. His dark hair was short and flecked with gray, although she doubted he was as old as he seemed.

"Umm, no. But thanks." Genie gazed at him. "You must be from Karin's side, then?"

He smiled slightly, just an uptick of his mouth. "I'm kind of from both sides. I'm Karin's ex, David, and Michael's best friend." He slipped his hand away.

Oh. My. God! This is David? He's gorgeous!

With cat-green eyes and a physique to make any girl swoon. Even better, he was taller than she. She couldn't control her exhalation. A tiny "oh," then she smiled.

The first real smile of the day.

"Hi, David. I'm Genie, one of Michael's mess mates."

CHAPTER 2

Genie was his messmate? She couldn't be 'Gene'?

Michael had always talked about how Gene was strong and capable. David had always assumed 'Gene' was a man. He hadn't really paid all that much attention to small details in the last few years.

Damn!

So 'Gene' was a gorgeous Amazon of a woman with streaky strawberry blonde hair, perfect breasts, strong and well defined muscles, and slate gray eyes.

His anatomy responded instantly at the awareness of her. With her height, she'd likely go nose to nose with most men, although she was shorter than he at his towering six foot five.

As she smiled, David noted the lush wide lips glossed with an icy pink. He wanted to taste them.

That was an eerily unfamiliar sensation for him.

"Err, who's your partner?" He looked around, hoping to hide just how flustered he really was.

"Danny. But he got called away. So I'm on my own."

He looked back at her, and she watched him in silence.

"Then, perhaps I could partner you?"

She blushed, a small crest of pink highlighting her cheeks. "That would be fabulous. Actually, I'd prefer not to be on the head table." Genie half-whispered the words, and he had to lean in, as the kiss of her sweet breath caressed his face.

He swallowed while his body woke from the sensual slumber it had existed in for so long. Liquid heat coursed through his veins as time slowed.

"And since Karin and Michael weren't after any real formality, it's not much of an issue today." She nodded to the round table in the center of the room, and he glanced over.

"Sure." He took her hand, slipping it through the crook of his arm. "So...you're the famous Gene."

She stiffened, and he cursed silently at her reaction. "I didn't know he ever talked about me."

David laughed at her peevish tone. "Geez, if I'd known you were a woman, I would've thought you another spoke in Michael's wheel." He cringed as soon as the words escaped.

What a stupid comment to make to a woman on her friend's wedding day!

"Well. Damn." Genie stopped stock-still, like an immovable object, and the small smile on her face grew wider. "He never said he talked about me. It was always Karin this, Karin that."

She's not upset. I didn't put my foot in it.

Inwardly he rejoiced, even though he was somewhat amazed at the strength of his reaction. Never before had he felt that instantaneous need to be doing the right thing with a woman.

Hell, even with Karin, it' been a case of '*this is me, take me or leave me*'.

With *this* woman, there was a subtle difference.

His mind shied away from the importance of that, unwilling to jinx whatever linked them together.

David laid a hand at the small of her back, noting idly the way her muscles tensed against his light touch, and he led her to a table at the edge of the room. "Does this suit you?"

She turned, and for a moment he was captured by her gaze.

"Oh. Yeah."

His mouth dried, tongue stuck to the roof of his mouth, and she smiled, heating his body further. "Great then." He couldn't drag his eyes away, and hers widened in recognition of the zing between them. Or so he hoped.

"There you are!" Gordon rounded the table, tugging Martine after him.

David had to control himself from lashing out in frustration, but the moment of connection had already passed.

"We thought we'd sit with you. Keep you company, you know?"

Instead of venting his frustration, he smiled blandly.

"Sure. Uh, have you met Gene? Genie?" He stumbled over the words, and Genie leaned in, taking Gordon's hand and shaking it firmly.

"And I'm Martine."

They sat down as the crowd flowed in, searching for seats, and he was thankful that the reception was so informal so he wouldn't need to share this time with anyone he didn't know or wasn't comfortable with.

"What are you doing?" Gordon whispered.

"Nothing. Just being sociable." He watched as Genie rose, excusing herself to use the powder room, the sway of her hips in the gown leaving his body tightly coiled.

"Dammit. Concentrate, man. You've come so far. Don't blow it now."

He turned, catching sight of the concern in Gordon's eyes. "What d'you mean?"

"I'm sure she's really nice, but is this really interest or just...you know? You haven't been in a relationship since... Dammit, you haven't even shown any interest in any woman since Karin," Martine whispered, and David shook his head.

"I don't know, but I'm interested for the first time in seeing where it leads."

Frustration about his state of mind— whether to feel thankful or pissed—bloomed.

He crossed his arms and waited for Genie's return.

GENIE SAT BESIDE THE MAN. *DAVID*. CONFUSION RAN through her system each time he moved. Each action caught her unaware, and she fought to make sense of her emotions.

She loved Michael, didn't she?

So why on earth was she so drawn to the man sitting beside her?

Each time she asked herself what it was about the man so close that drew her like a magnet, but the answer continued to elude her.

And I don't like being unable to name my emotions.

The speeches and meal passed quickly enough; not that she could name anything she ate. Genie didn't care, as she listened to the cadence of David's voice.

He eschewed the wine she noticed, in favor of water and soft drinks, a small fact that she filed away to question later.

Then came the dancing. The bride and groom rose and started waltzing, and David laid a soft hand on hers. "Join me?"

Her stomach quivered with a million butterflies, but she nodded, more than eager to see what it felt like to be in his arms.

They stood, and Genie smoothed down the dress, tugging at the bodice once more.

"You aren't comfortable?" He quirked an eyebrow, assumed a pose and she sighed.

"I don't usually do dresses."

He smiled, and her limbs softened while her heartbeat accelerated. "You look fantastic in that one."

"Thanks." She gulped, hearing a promise in his voice. What it was a promise of, she wanted to explore.

Later. Maybe we'll have a chance to talk and learn more after the reception.

That idea got her upright and kept her that way.

He steered her smoothly on the floor, her body snug against his.

A moan escaped as his hand settled at the base of her spine as tingles and a whole lot more beside tempted her. Thoughts of naughty sexy things began rolling through Genie's mind.

The kind that required two naked adults, plus time and privacy and her panties dampened at some of the more X-rated things.

"You're ... You're a wonderful dancer." She managed the words, but they sounded forced.

David laughed, and her body shivered as nerve endings quivered. His soft breath whispered over her bare shoulder.

"Do you want to stay here?" he murmured the words, and she shook her head slightly.

"Not really. Let's go find somewhere to talk."

His hands fell from her body, and she felt that loss keenly, but instead he linked his fingers through hers.

She stopped.

"Bag? Keys?" he whispered.

Clutch. Where had she left her clutch? Her mind moved slowly recalling the small cloakroom, where she had lodged those items earlier in the day.

"In the...in the cloakroom."

"Good." He dragged her over to Michael and Karin, their hands entwined. "Guys. Congrats. I really mean that."

The bride, threw her arms around David, and for a moment Genie felt a twinge of jealousy. Then as she pulled away she heard her whisper. "Thank you for coming, David. I'm so glad we're still friends. You know how much it means to me." Then the woman swept her up in a hug. "He's a good man. Just...be kind to him."

The words confused Genie.

What on earth are they supposed to mean?

As she pulled away, she noted the sheen of tears in the bride's eyes. "Congrats, Karin and Michael. I know you'll do really well together."

Michael moved in. "She's so great and I'm so lucky. I hope you find that one day soon, too." He tugged her close, enveloped her in a quick and hard hug before releasing her. Genie's gaze landed on David.

Even as she stood back her mind whispered, can it really be this simple?

Could it be true that the man she thought she loved wasn't really the right one? Could *David* be the one she needed?

A sense of disquiet filled her and she batted it away. Genie wasn't looking for deep and mysterious today.

"Thanks for coming. We'll catch up when we get back." Michael's gaze held hers for a moment. Then he glanced down, noting the way they were holding hands and winked. "Good work, Gene." He flashed his hundred watt smile.

Turning away, she focused on the warmth and zing from the touch of the man holding her hand.

The change is in me.

She was startled and stopped; gripped David's hand tighter, feeling the warmth in his touch and that sense of reassurance.

He looked back at her and smiled. His smile nearly stopped her heart, and when he tugged gently, she followed.

"The cloakroom," she muttered as he hurried her through the mass of bodies writhing in time to the music.

Once past the threshold of the room, he turned, whirling her into his arms.

"If you don't want this, tell me now. Because, God knows, I do." David's words didn't contain any of the veneer of sophistication he'd shown earlier.

Instead, they were rough and hungry. It was clear in the tight grip and his unsteady words that his desire matched her own.

Thought vanished as he moved in to meet her lips

CHAPTER 3

Warm. Mobile. Lush.

Myriad emotions ricocheted through his mind. She tasted amazing. When her lips opened he let his tongue surge in, mating with hers.

Genie groaned, and he swallowed the sound, grateful when her arms reached up around his neck as he slipped his own around her waist.

More and closer, his body demanded as she bowed her body against his. His mind blanked. Her satin covered chest rested against him. The blood pounded through his body, and his erection pressed for satisfaction.

He pulled away, panting for breath and he fought to clear his mind. *Too much. Too fast.* Their connection, if he could call it that, demanded so much more but slower than this current urges begged for.

"We have to stop." David's voice sounded hoarse, even to his own dazed mind. He glanced at her, and the flush on her chest and cheeks, the heavy eyes also spoke of her desire. It filled him with a mixture of hope and regret.

The memory of the concern he'd read in Martine and

Gordon's eyes played at the edges of his consciousness. He tried to brush it aside, but it remained there, like an irritating stone in a shoe, rubbing and abrading at his nerves.

Regret that they couldn't continue this tryst right now filled him, but they had to stop. Anyone could come around the corner and see them.

He wouldn't give in to the urge to ravish her here, where anyone could see. That would cheapen whatever happened *next*.

No.

If this was going to go further, it wo*uld be* on their terms.

Slowly and in the right location. With both of them agreeing to anything that might take place.

"Let's get out of here." Genie dragged him to the cloakroom and grabbed her small bag and wrap and hauled him down the steps. "Your car or mine?"

His face flushed with heat. "I don't have a car."

She stopped and quirked an eye*brow at him.*

God, how can I tell her?

David gathered every bit of bravado and plunged. "I'm an alcoholic. Recovering. I don't have a car because I lost my license."

"Oh. Darn." She stopped and looked at him, her eyes carefully blank. "That would be a bummer."

He grimaced. The flame that'd roared within his chest, warming him through, flickered and died. Any hope of a relationship with her was over before it began. What woman wanted to be with an alcoholic? Recovering or not, it wasn't something most women felt comfortable with. He might as well leave now.

"Where're you going?" She sounded perplexed, and he looked over his shoulder.

"Umm, leaving you so you don't..." His gut churned.

"What? After that hot kiss? I don't think so, buddy boy." Genie's brash attitude dropped away, exposing a vulnerability she clearly hid well.

She wasn't as brash or confident as the front she showed the world. Shame filled him, that he'd so carelessly formed such an opinion without even giving her a chance.

"I thought... Umm. Sorry. I must have read it wrong." She blushed deeply and started to back away, fishing in her small bag with jerky moves.

"Wait." David couldn't help himself. He touched her shoulder, and she stopped, refused to look at him, and instead Genie went an even deeper scarlet.

"It's all good. Honestly." An ache started in the region of his heart.

"No, it's not. It's me. I thought..."

She stopped and lifted her eyes.

"I thought you wouldn't want to be with me after you heard the truth," his confession slipped out.

Her mouth fell open as she dropped the body of the bag, holding on by the long cord straps. "Not want... Why?" Her eyes grew larger. "Because you're a recovering alcoholic?" She breathed deeply, shuddering a little. "I'm not so small that I'd run away because of that." Genie moved forward and grabbed his hand, squeezing it tightly. "Maybe we better go for a drive and talk. Get to know each other."

David nodded, unable to speak as she towed him to her car, but the cold numb area in the region of his chest warmed a little once more.

She drove a sweet little dark blue convertible, and if he was correct, was of vintage age. He climbed in, watching as she stowed the bag in the glove compartment and handed him her wrap. Genie's movements were slow and measured even as she started the car. The indicator clacked away, and she pulled out of the parking lot, joined the traffic and headed north.

They didn't drive far, only to a nearby coffee shop.

"This do for now?"

He nodded, watching as she parked smoothly.

"We can get some coffees, then head back to my place or down to the river. You pick." Her voice was breathless as if she'd just run *a race.*

David's stomach jittered. Her place. What would it be like?

Perfect and neat, or messy but homely, like Karin had always attempted to create?

They moved together ordering mocha lattes to go and waited in silence. They stood close, but their connection, if he could even call it that, was too new to allow for much small talk between them. Their fingers twined, neither willing to let the other go.

The discussion he desired to have wasn't suited to this location, and heat swept through him. He didn't doubt she felt it as strongly as he did, with her measured glances, and light touches, the blush on her cheeks and shallow breathing. The way her eyes shone. It paint*ed the picture of a wo*man who wanted.

Could I be that lucky?

The woman behind the counter finally called them over handing over the two insulated cups, and they left.

"Where to?" Genie broke the silence.

David took a deep breath. "Your place."

She smiled. "Good."

CHAPTER 4

Genie led him up the steps, the house old but lovingly restored. Balustrades gleamed a rich dark chestnut brown, and he ran his hands along them, feeling the silky smoothness of the wood beneath his fingers. She opened the door, and he stepped in to a cool room.

The pale tones caught his eyes first, everything perfectly harmonious. Not new, the covers on the chairs showed some wear here and there, but they were immaculately clean. Simple blinds graced the windows letting in lots of light, and the scent of fresh cut flowers filled the air.

Even with the old furniture, it screamed out fresh and cared for.

He smiled.

She carried an air of freshness about her. It was something intangible he hadn't come across in a very long time, and for a moment, he frowned.

Was that part of the reason he'd lost his way?

"Make yourself comfortable." She sipped from her cup as she watched him.

Squirming under her gaze, David shed his good black

shoes and left them by the front door before wandering into the lounge, and, finding a spot in one of the armchairs he lowered himself into it.

Drinking deeply of the coffee he allowed himself time to clear his mind. Then the last drop was gone as was his excuse to simply be.

"I'm just going to change. I'll be back." Genie smiled weakly.

Did she regret inviting him back to her home? That sat badly with him, but he remained silent as she disappeared.

He waited, the nerves in his fingers and arms jumping a little. What was she doing?

David imagined her peeling the gown from her body, her breasts springing free. Would her nipples be shell pink or darker tones of chocolate?

His erection jerked, and he moved a hand down to the front of his pants, shifting slightly and sighed.

A soft tread behind him caught his attention. There she stood, in a light blue top and jeans. "Thanks for waiting." Genie smiled and sat down on the sofa opposite, tucking her bare feet up beneath her. "That must have been odd today, watching Karin marry Michael."

He took a moment to consider the implicit query in her comment. "A little. But they're good for each other. Karin needed something I didn't have, after Emma Rose died. Michael was there supporting her. Hell, he supported me half the time, too."

She watched him in silence.

Before anything could happen, he needed to give her a chance to walk away. He wasn't perfect, but he was stronger than before. "After Emma Rose died, we kind of fell apart. I realize now, looking back, she was the glue that held us together. I doubt we would've lasted even if she'd lived. It was a painful process coming to terms with that reality." David shrugged. "Karin and I are much better as friends than lovers." A lump formed in his throat. If this was as important as he hoped, then they needed an honest foundation. "I wanted to have it all. A family and get ahead with my career."

Genie listened quietly, nodding.

"I was a lawyer on the fast train up. I had what everyone called, a stable and committed relationship with Karin, a beautiful daughter. A house overlooking the water in the very best suburb and near great schools." He stopped, needing a moment to recoup as the reminder of what he'd lost battered at him. "My future seemed assured."

"Then Emma Rose got sick?" she prompted quietly.

"Yes. Then we found out Emma Rose had a rare form of leukemia. One that didn't respond to the common treatments for the illness. What we didn't know at the time, was that we had less than twelve months left with her."

Genie leaned forward touching a hand to his leg. "You don't have to..."

"I do. You need to know it all." David smiled. It was a mere shadow, and less than a grimace. "I took time off work. Stayed home when I could to help Karin, but slowly Emma Rose faded away on us. Once she was hospitalized, it was like I was holding on with fingernails. Excruciating, knowing I couldn't do anything but be with her." The pain bloomed large and heavy in his chest, choking the life from him again. "Then she passed on."

He stopped, needing to regroup, dragging in a lungful of air as his eyes burned with unshed tears. "Karin and I...we just didn't have anything except the pain between us left. I started drinking. It numbed everything, you know? One drink became two. That became a bottle, then two or three.

I was searching for a way to run away from life, but it just made things so much worse. Then I got done for drunk driving." He laughed, hearing the mirthless sound, unable to contain his feelings of shame. "Being a lawyer did no good, but the judge was fair. He took my license and my car; gave me an order to go to AA." David closed his eyes, not wanting to see the shock on her face. "I lost my job, too, so I couldn't pay the mortgage, and Karin left me. My life was falling apart, and I couldn't cope."

"Karin was suffering, too." Genie's gentle words allowed him to share his secret shame.

"Yes. Karin was suffering, and I could see it, but my own pain... It overwhelmed me. I couldn't cope with *mine*, let alone hers. So rather than be there for her, I wasn't even there for me." He grimaced and his eyes burned. "In the last twelve months or so, Michael's family helped me find a way out of the bottom of the bottle. Michael, Martine, and even Gordon, took me to the AA meetings. It was around then I realized Michael and Karin had hooked up. They're good for each other. While I miss her on one level, it wasn't a love that would've held us together. That was what Emma Rose did for us."

"You must miss her."

His eyes opened, understanding she was talking about Emma Rose, not Karin.

"Every day. She truly was the light of my life. But I have to go on. Live my life again. Learn to do without her." David rose, moved next to Genie and lowered himself onto the sofa.

She shifted along, just enough to allow him room.

"But what about you and Michael?" he asked.

Genie blushed, dipped her head for a moment and twisted her hands together.

He was thankful that she let him change the subject without pushing any further.

"I thought I loved him. Thought we belonged together. But I realize now, it was nothing more than a dream and wish on my part. He's my friend, but was never meant to be my lover." She smiled, reaching out with a shaking hand and cupped his cheek.

Her touch burned him, and he quelled the gasp that would have escaped at her touch.

"He and Karin do belong together, and that was simply one of the biggest issues for me. I felt like such a fraud there today." She laughed a little, but it, too, carried no humor. "I could see up there, today, just how much they belonged together. And yet I still had this grain of jealousy eating at me. Now I just feel ill, thinking about it." She sighed.

"It makes you normal." David leaned forward, placing one hand on her jean-clad leg. "It makes you honest, too."

She shifted forward ready to meet him.

"It makes you perfect ... to me." He reached in until their lips met, and heat exploded through him.

Genie settled back, her fingers playing over her lips as she smiled a little, her eyes downcast and focusing on of the denim covering her legs.

His secrets and hers had been aired, and now they had an opportunity to move forward, to determine if there was a possibility of a relationship. Instinct told her this man was truly stronger than any she'd ever met.

Emotionally, he'd gained that strength from the terrible tragedy of losing his daughter and everything he'd built.

How quickly she'd reached that conclusion, too. "I don't

want you to leave," Genie whispered, and he smiled gently.

David hadn't turned away when she'd told him of her own petty jealousies. Instead he'd understood, and for that alone thankfulness filled her.

She closed her eyes letting his touch fill her mind, his fingers soft and gentle on her leg. She raised shaking fingers, covering his briefly and rubbing her thumb over the calluses on his hands.

His own movements stilled for a second, and Genie opened her eyes, hoping he could see the invitation shining there for him.

He leaned in. "I'm not going anywhere if you want me to stay."

She let questing fingers trail down the broad chest hidden by the black coat. "Maybe you should get more comfortable, though."

The tones of a cellphone trilled, and David pulled away regretfully.

She searched his face, detecting a hint of impatience at the intrusion. "Just let me get this."

He answered the tiny device, while Genie blocked out the sounds of him talking, instead focusing on calming herself.

She rose, then took the empty to go cups to the kitchen, quickly dipping her fingers under the running water of the tap. She wiped the dampness over her cheeks and breathed deeply, before returning to the room and her spot on the couch.

He'd hung up and frowned at the phone before shoving it back into his pocket. "Now then..."

"You need to get more comfortable."

David smiled, and her stomach somersaulted deep inside as she lifted her hands to his jacket.

He grinned as she helped him push the material away, revealing the pristine white shirt below.

It covered the skin she wanted to reveal and touch. Once his jacket lay over the back of the seat, she toyed with a button.

He yanked on the tie, letting it loosen, and Genie carefully unfastened it then slowly unclipped one button after another, revealing the bronzed skin below. "You're so tanned. What do you do now?"

David let out a laugh. "I work in a nursery. It's very relaxing. I'm also studying garden design. Who knows? Maybe that's really where my talents lie?"

She giggled. "No wonder you have such beautiful muscles. I like a guy with a firm body."

"Then I'm your man."

Genie stilled as his words filtered through her. "I think you could be." She rose up on her knees and swayed toward him.

He caught her up in his arms, her fingers brushing over his shoulders and down his back, taking his shirt with them, while his reached for the hem of her top and pulled it up.

Their kiss fired her senses and left her reeling as her body melted against his.

She pulled away, needing oxygen, and David hauled the shirt up over her head, leaving her lurching slightly in jeans and bra.

"I need to see you." His guttural words sent her pulse racing harder, and her nipples ached for his touch.

Genie reached behind and fumbled with the clips, finding them and pulling the offending fabric to one side, holding the clasp for an instant as she watched his eyes darken. She released her grip, and the bra fluttered to the floor forgotten.

His hands settled over the aching mounds, and with infinite care, his thumbs traced the distended nubs. "So beautiful."

Her secret recesses melted as he touched and worshipped her body, his fingers releasing her and trailing down her stomach and finding the small belly button ring that she hid most of the time.

He fondled it for a moment while she gasped before he found the fasteners for her jeans.

One hand moved to her shoulder and pushed her back into the deep cushions of the chair, and she moved slowly, the whole time her eyes watching his, which were now hooded with desire for her.

David pushed the heavy material down her legs, and she lifted her hips. He hissed.

Genie lay there bare except for a scrap of lace that almost covered her.

"Exquisite."

Now she wanted, needed the same. She reached for his waistband, but he pushed her hands away.

"Not yet," he whispered.

He lowered his body over hers, his flat nipples rubbing hers, and her breath hitched.

"Oh God!"

She arched away as his fingers found the way under the elastic of her panties. "Wet just for me." His quiet words and gentle stroking touches nearly sent her over the edge, and David placed his lips against hers.

She opened to him as he stroked across her sensitive folds.

The sweet torture continued as he pulled away and slid down her body, leveling his mouth with her nipples. Then he opened and suckled on the engorged flesh.

Genie cried out. She couldn't stop it as a single finger dipped within her molten core and his tongue flicked against her. "David!"

He moved, swirling and dancing his digit deep within her, and the fire grew hotter and wilder.

Her hips moved, but she didn't care as her body screamed for release. "Please!"

David moved to the other breast, whispering against her flesh. "Enjoying that, are we?"

She couldn't formulate an answer as his lips began the process once again, and his hand continued its intimate caress.

One finger became two, and movements were more urgent as her hands tangled in his hair, yanking him away.

"Dammit! More. Now. More!" Her breathless entreaties had him slipping away, tearing at the pale pink panties.

They shredded and flew over his shoulder as David shoved himself to his knees, widening her thighs, then his mouth was there. Sucking and licking until she burned with wild need.

"Don't. Stop!" Genie cried and moaned, legs moving wildly as her body bucked.

The warmth grew, burgeoning within her until she finally splintered, screaming his name as he lapped at her.

Then it was over, and she lay in a boneless heap on the couch. "You ...you. Didn't..."

David raised his head from between her knees. "Not yet."

Genie tugged him to her, but he shook his head. "I don't have any condoms. I don't suppose you do either?"

He looked so boyish, but she shook her head.

"No." She wailed the word, but he smiled.

"Soon. Not yet, but definitely soon. I don't think either of us is ready for that, just yet, anyway. We need to know each other better."

David gathered her into his arms tenderly, and Genie lay there as her body slowed, and finally she fell asleep cocooned within his embrace.

She'd been a surprise, in more ways than one. She'd allowed him to love her and had responded wholeheartedly to his touches.

The phone call he'd tried to ignore kept worrying at him.

Gordon had called, worried he was about to make some kind of mistake and he'd assume some kind of connection between them was more than it was. His former brother-in-law had mentioned David's enchantment might be too much too soon.

In the end, he'd promised Gordon he wouldn't make any rash decisions, based on a single day's acquaintance.

"Gordon, my friend, if only you understood," he murmured as he gazed down at the sleeping woman. "I'm *already* in over my head."

Sure, he understood their concern.

After all, the last year or two had been horrific. He'd made a number of bad decisions, lacked any kind of conscience about the ramifications of his actions.

A skittering breeze grazed him, and David closed his eyes. The mixed fragrances of vanilla and chocolate caught him before they floated away, and he allowed sleep to claim him.

CHAPTER 5

Genie woke slowly, stretching. An unfamiliar warmth surrounded her. A weight draped across her waist, and she carefully eased herself up.

David was lying behind her, fast asleep snuggled under the blanket in her bed.

With me, and I'm naked. We're both naked!

Memories of the passionate encounter from the night before flooded her mind.

Well damn.

That was probably the best loving of her whole entire life, and *he'd* given it. In spades. Taking nothing for himself.

She carefully lowered herself back down and snuggled against him, enjoying the warm strength of his body against hers, while a soft male snuffle sounded in her ears. "I could get used to this," she whispered.

"So could I." David's drowsy words had her tensing, before she gave into a smile.

His hand slipped up and down her arm, arousing her as much as offering support. "We should get up. See what time it is." For a second, she hoped he'd disagree, enjoying the closeness, but he sighed and pulled back the covers.

"I know."

Genie crawled to the side of the bed and swung her legs over, a little embarrassed by her nudity, and heat stained her cheeks.

David moved behind her. "Don't be embarrassed. You're gorgeous, and I'm looking forward to making love with you."

His mouth nibbled along her shoulder, and she shivered as her body ignited once more.

She couldn't control the hungry moan, and she turned to capture his mouth rapaciously, urgently letting their tongues mate as soon as he opened to her.

Hands roamed, gliding over naked flesh and gripping tight.

He pulled away, panting slightly. "We need to stop, or we...I won't be able to." Desire flickered in his eyes, filling her with womanly triumph.

"Soon. Don't make me wait too long." She moved away, grabbing up the old dressing gown on the end of the bed and pulling it around her body. "Coffee?"

He smiled and nodded, and she padded off to the kitchen.

So new, yet she could swear this was love at first sight. God, how she hoped the relationship would live up to what it promised.

Her conscience prompted caution. She'd been wrong before—with Michael.

What if she was again?

Genie took a deep breath, ignoring the sharp barb of uncertainty and filled the kettle.

THEY SPENT THE DAY TOGETHER, SHARING TALES FROM their daily lives, and he let himself soak up the warmth of her company.

Genie had suggested a drive to the beach, and David had eagerly agreed. They'd packed an impromptu picnic, before she'd driven them to a secluded cove.

"How did you know this was here?" He couldn't contain the surprise in his voice.

She laughed, a full-throated sound that heated him through.

"I used to live not too far from here. My parents were pseudo-hippies. They both worked nine to five, but had these dreams of buying a kombi and driving around the country. Needless to say, that wasn't possible with four children in tow."

David stared. "Four children?"

She nodded. "Yeah, I know. You have Zeta, Agamemnon, Hercules, and me. I was the youngest, by a lot. The other three were at school, and they realized how difficult their naming preferences were by the time I arrived on scene. So I got Gene." Genie grinned. "I'm just pleased they got the weird names out of their system by the time I was born. Otherwise, I could've been Aphrodite or Parthenope."

"You are kidding about the names, aren't you?" He chuckled, and she shook her head.

"Nope."

With a last quick laugh, David pulled the blanket into position and set down the basket, watching as she lowered herself to the mat.

"So what did they do for work?" He wanted to know everything about her.

"Dad was an auto electrician. Mum was a retail assistant. Neither of them wanted to go to university. They were happily married for thirty odd years, until Dad died of a heart attack four years ago."

"Are you close to your family?" The concept of happy families eluded him, his own having been a case of largely absent parents, and while he'd been close to Michael, he had no experience of siblings.

"Oh they're all out there, saving the world or making money. Zeta is in London working for a financial institution. Mum and Dad were horrified when she brought home the paperwork for university and said she wanted to make money. Dad ranted for days about how it was evil and we should all live on mung beans and fish." She giggled. "He was even more upset when I enlisted. I think we females of the family let him down severely. Herc and Ag ... they went off and studied, too. Herc is a vet. He reckons animals never tease him because of his silly name. Ag is working on a station in Western Australia, somewhere." Genie's voice was filled with affection. Her face glowed.

She was a woman who loved deeply.

She whipped open the basket and started lifting out the salads and cold meats they'd packed. "What about you? Do you have brothers or sisters?"

David shook his head. "No. Mum and Dad never really wanted kids. I was a surprise. Mum's a corporate lawyer, and Dad's a professor. We get together regularly, but..."

She stilled, and in her eyes he could read sorrow.

With one hand, Genie rubbed his in a gesture of understanding. "I'm so sorry. It must've been lonely."

For the first time, he understood that was the reason he'd wanted his marriage to Karin to work.

Emma Rose had been the icing on the cake, but he'd wanted a family more than he'd loved Karin and wanted a wife. They'd stuck it out for their daughter...but once she was gone, there was nothing to keep them together.

"Karin, Michael, and I all grew up together. I can't think of a time when I didn't know them or hang out at Karin's or Michael's place. When Gordon married Martine, she just became part of the team. Michael was away a lot in the last few years, as you know, with the Army. That's when Karin and I finally got together."

A lump formed in his throat, and he looked out to the sea, watching the gentle roll of waves lapping at the shore. The call of the seabirds soothed him, and when he looked back, Genie smiled, allowing him to set the pace.

"I guess we should eat."

She nodded silently, and the emotions swelled inside David once more.

CHAPTER 6

Nervousness filled Genie as she smoothed down the black pants. He was taking her over to Gordon and Martine's for a barbeque. David had told her they'd been his most staunch supporters through Emma Rose's illness and his subsequent battle with alcohol.

Her stomach quivered as she waited for him to open the door of his small apartment. It wasn't in a great location, but he'd explained despite his parents offering him a spot in their home, he'd needed a space of his own.

The squeak of the metal hinges cut through her thoughts.

"Hi. Sorry I'm late. The guys only dropped me back twenty minutes ago. The delivery was late, and we had to unload the truck…" His words died away, and the heat in his eyes warmed her. "You look amazing!"

She grinned. "You don't look too bad yourself." Her fingers itched to reach out and brush the errant lock of hair that'd fallen over his brow. "We better get moving, otherwise…" Genie winked, and he barked a laugh.

"Promises, promises!" David snagged one of her hands, pulling her close.

The scent of him rose around her, and she struggled to breathe through the growing need clawing at her belly.

In the three weeks since they'd got together they'd both waited, but oh man! It was hard. She snorted and he silently questioned her.

Genie shook her head and closed the distance between them. Their lips met in a gentle touch but it was enough to ignite the fire that'd remained banked since the night they'd met. Her hand rose, cupping his muscled shoulder through the cotton of his shirt.

David pulled back. "Let's get out of here," he muttered, then tugged her along, down the path to the roadside where she'd parked and insisted on opening the car door for her.

She climbed in and waited for him to settle himself. The click of the seatbelt was audible over the whirr of the motor, and she smoothly drew away from the curve.

He'd already showed her where they were going, so she concentrated on the road, knowing that for David, this was a huge step. Not only would Gordon and Martine be there, but also Karin and Michael, back fresh from their brief honeymoon.

It was akin to meeting the parents, and her palms were sweaty slick against the steering wheel as she maneuvered into the driveway of the tidy brick house. "Do I look okay?" Her hands went to her hair as he leaned in, placing a quick kiss on her still kiss-plumped lips.

"You look fantastic. Now let's get round the back." He waited as she closed the car door before ushering her to a hidden wooden gate and across a rock and paver path.

Behind the house she could smell meats cooking on a wood fire and the sounds of voices.

As they rounded the corner, there were cries of welcome, and she sucked in a deep breath. *God, I hope they like me.*

Michael and Karin waved, and acquaintances with Gordon and Martine were renewed.

David watched them all.

Genie chatted happily to Michael and Karin. She engaged with Martine and Gordon, but he could tell how nervous she was.

The way she gripped her fingers together. The scuff she made with the ball of her foot, changing from one to the other.

Gordon and Martine kept asking questions, and made comments about the long-standing friendship among the five of them, and David kept his thoughts to himself. Something about the situation just felt wrong.

"So, you two are an item?" Martine smiled, but he couldn't detect anything other than surface interest.

He frowned.

"Martine..."

She laid a soft hand on his arm, and he wanted to pull away. "Now, come on, David. We've known you a long time. Let's get to know Genie."

Unease slithered through him. This wasn't the normal way Martine behaved.

"After all, with everything..."

"Martine." He growled, and she stopped and patted his cheek.

"Come on. Lighten up a little." His former sister-in-law

grinned and leaned forward to Genie. "Would you like a drink?"

Her words had him stiffening, and Genie shifted anxious eyes to him. "No. I'm good with a soda, thanks."

The knot in his belly tightened. What the hell was Martine up to?

"You only met at the wedding, didn't you?" Gordon called from the barbeque, and Genie nodded.

"Umm, yes. But I've known Michael for years and heard all about David. Little did I know..."

Her words died away, and he willed her to continue, but instead she shrugged.

"Well, you know how it is." She grinned weakly, and it left him deflated.

Did she feel the connection he did, or was it just a figment of his imagination?

"Meat's cooked!" Gordon announced, and Martine stood up.

"Oh dear me, I haven't brought the plates out yet," she admitted.

Karin made to stand, but Martine fluttered over. "Stay where you are. Rest your legs. Maybe Genie will help?" She cocked her eyebrow, and Genie nodded, rising, then followed Martine inside.

Karin excused herself quickly, and concern flashed through David.

What the hell was going on?

"David. Can we talk frankly? Martine and I are concerned."

David turned toward Gordon. "What about?"

"It's ... you know, we're concerned about you. How quickly this has..." Gordon looked away, a red crest on his cheeks.

"Look, Genie's great. But she's a long term bet," Michael spoke quietly, lifting his drink. "She's a keeper, and you've had a rough time. We're worried about you. About how quickly you've developed this relationship."

Anger grew, but he restrained it. "So you think…"

"We don't want you to backslide. Just the same as we don't want to see Genie hurt either. You're both good people. We just … have concerns. That's all."

"Never once did I question *you*, Michael, when things between you and *my ex* became hot and heavy. And Gordon, when you went through that rough patch with Martine, I was there. Supporting you. That's what friends do." He breathed heavily.

How could they question my feelings?

Michael stepped closer, but he shook his head.

"This is our *private* business. I had hoped you'd be pleased Genie and I are together. That my life is finally back on track. Instead I get *this*." He waved to them and the house.

They both blushed a deep red.

"If you're my friends, then you'll be happy for us. Stand with us. Otherwise…" David was unable to continue, but they nodded, obviously understanding exactly what he meant.

He rose, but even as he did, the sliding door between the house and patio area opened.

Martine followed by Genie headed for the table, and he subsided.

"Later. We can talk about this later. "

CHAPTER 7

Genie wanted to curl up in a corner. Damn, Martine had seemed so nice at the wedding. But tonight... Well, if she didn't miss her guess, the warning signs were just about battering her over the head.

So when Martine requested her help in the kitchen, she wasn't surprised. They'd entered the house, and she'd commented on how lovely the rooms were. When Karin entered after them, she'd scented an ambush.

"So. You and David, huh? He's a great guy." Karin's words had laid the groundwork for the attack.

"Yeah. He's a special kind of guy."

Martine had thrust a tomato into her hand. "Can you cut this please?"

Genie had nodded and started slicing.

"You know he's had a really rough time of it. Both he and Karin have struggled in the last few years."

She hadn't wanted to discuss it but nodded in silence, hoping to head it off at the pass.

"Yeah, after the issues he's had to work through, we're concerned that nothing drag him back down now he's finally getting on top again." Martine had popped a glass bowl at Genie's elbow. "He's come a long way. Had to work hard to get where he is now. He's settled."

"I know. He told me."

"Has he?" The question in Karin's voice had her head turning toward the woman. "So you know about the alcohol. His license?"

Genie nodded again. She really didn't want to discuss this.

Instead, she focused on the job, covering the slices with film and hoping they'd stop. Bit her lip until it stung in order to remain silent.

"We care about him. We don't want to see him hurt. If you aren't in this for the long term, then you need to cut it now. Because we won't just let someone pull him apart. He's come too far."

Genie closed her eyes at Karin's words.

What do they think I'm going to do? Have sex with him and then dump him? Is that what they think?

Her breath caught in her throat.

"Look, all we're saying is this. If you're serious, take it slowly. After all, there's no rush, is there?" Martine gazed at her then nodded. "Now, we'd better get this stuff outside to the men, before they come looking for us."

"Wait."

They stopped and looked back at her.

"Whatever we decide to do is between us—and I know you're worried about him—it will be our decision. I'm worried about him, too, and will never intentionally hurt him." Tears burned in throat. "I care for him. Deeply. But you have to understand, this is *our* business."

Neither woman spoke. Instead they watched her as she

struggled to find her balance once more. "I get that you're concerned, but what is between us is just that. *Between us.*"

The silence grew.

"Please. Let us find our own way."

The women nodded in silence. An understanding had been reached and Genie mechanically loaded up the tray with the salads and vegetables, listening as Karin and Martine loaded the other with crockery and cutlery.

Their comments stung. How could they think that of her, without actually knowing what was going on?

THE TRIP HOME WAS QUIET.

"Did you want to stay?" Her voice was almost inaudible, and he sighed.

She hadn't been overly communicative since before the meal. Something had occurred inside. Had they ambushed her? Given her the third degree?

David needed to find out, because unless he did, their fragile relationship could be destroyed.

"Not really, no."

He watched as she drove, the grip of her fingers on the steering wheel, the way she carefully avoided looking at him, all made him experience a mixture of anger, regret, and hurt.

"So." Genie turned towards him briefly before returning her gaze to the road ahead.

"So," she echoed. "You've got really good friends. They care a lot about you." She cleared her throat.

"Dammit..."

"Can this wait 'til we get home?"

Passing under a light, he caught the glimpse of a tear balanced on her eyelashes and instantly felt gutted.

"Yeah." David settled back in his seat, but inside tension coiled.

She nodded and drove finally turning into her street, indicating and parking.

They climbed out, and he waited as Genie secured her vehicle and led the way upstairs and through the door, into the welcoming room.

He reached out, but she danced away from him.

"We need to talk."

Those death-knell words crashed into him, and his gut clenched. "What do you mean, we need to talk?"

She paled at the tone in his voice. A solitary tear streaked down her face. "Your friends don't think I'm good for you. They want us to slow down and…"

He moved. Couldn't stop himself as he reached her. "No. Don't say anymore." David kissed her. Hard and needy. He infused every fear and every want into it, crushing her to him.

When he pulled away, they both breathed harshly.

"I don't think I can walk away from this. From you. I don't know for sure what I'm feeling, but trust me. I'm not letting you go without being damned sure we've both given this thing between us everything we have."

Genie burst into tears, and he held her close. "I don't want you to let me go."

He smiled as she wailed, but the brief flash of happiness dissipated quickly. "They're worried I'll backslide. That one or both of us will be hurt."

She nodded, hiccupped and wiped the tears away with the heels of her hands. "I know."

He hugged her close to him again.

"Should we slow down?" she asked.

"Why don't we just wait and see where this goes? Let it happen in its own time?" David whispered against her shining cap of hair, inhaling the fragrance of Genie. The one he craved daily.

She nodded again, and he kissed her softly on the lips.

CHAPTER 8

David wiped the sweat from his brow and checked his watch again. Genie overdue by more than fifteen minutes. In the five weeks they'd been together, she'd never been late, not even once, to pick him up from work.

His gut told him everything was fine, but his mind remembered the sense of loss he'd experienced when Emma Rose passed away, and the memory ate away at him. He bit out a savage oath and picked up the gardening implement again, hoping that the physical activity would keep his mind from his concern. He swung it over his shoulder and punched it into the dirt with an *oomph*.

Five weeks, two days.

Countless nights of heavy petting had left him aroused all day. Every day.

The promise in this relationship built within him.

She was the one.

The only one he wanted to be with. His other half. His heart and soul. The guys on the job had stopped wolf-whistling her every day when she drove up after the first week.

He smiled as he recalled the way she blushed at the attention.

They were a great band of guys to work with. David had learned so much and had nearly finished his term with the company.

Last night he'd told Genie of his plans to open his own garden design company. She'd been enthusiastic and asked him if he'd like to begin on her yard. The truth was, he wanted her yard to be *their* yard.

His rented place had a cold empty feel to it, after being in Genie's home. Sharing her bed had become an almost nightly occurrence, yet they hadn't slept together in the biblical sense.

Tonight, though, he hoped to change that. They'd both agreed that they wanted to be ready for that final intimacy.

David patted his jeans pocket. He'd bought supplies, hoping tonight would be the night.

The sound of a purring engine pulled him from his reverie. There she was, scowling but very much intact, as she turned off the engine and crawled out of the car.

"Everything okay?"

She looked up and smiled, the instant transformation of her face breathtaking to watch. She strode over and placed both hands on his shoulders, leaning in for a kiss that would have peeled paint off the pick handle, if there'd been any left.

"Idiot C.O.s. Nothing too serious."

He nuzzled her cheek before pulling away. "Just let me get rid of this and grab my bag. Then we can go."

Genie nodded, pulling back and shading her eyes while he carried the pick over to the secure storage container, then wiped down quickly with the towel they kept handy.

He snatched up his backpack and loped back to where she waited. "Right, let's get out of here. I need a shower."

She let out a bark of laughter. "Just kind of...you need to stop the mud wrestling."

David snickered, throwing his gear onto the back seat and climbing in to the car. As always he marveled at how much care and attention she lavished on her car, the toweling cover she'd bought for his seat, so he wouldn't fret about making a mess in it. He loved that she took such great care of him and was prepared to make adjustments to her life so he felt not just included, but necessary.

A quick drive in quiet traffic brought them to her house, and she threw him the keys so he could open the door and go inside.

"Need some help?" he called, seeing her pulling some shopping carriers from the boot.

Genie shook her head with a smile.

He headed for the bathroom, pulling off his clothes as he went, looking forward to the feeling of the water washing away the grime and sweat accumulated in a day of hard work. He pulled open the screen, stepped inside, and turned on the water, waiting for the steam to rise as he ducked under the spray.

A sound caught his attention, and an arm snaked around his midsection just as he started to turn. His erection was at attention in an instant once more as the fingers roamed over his body. "Genie?"

"Who else, lover boy?"

David groaned as her lips found the muscles at his back, each touch heating him from the outside in, branding him as hers. Unable to wait any longer, he turned. "Do you have any idea how much I want you? How much I want *this*?"

She laughed, deep and throaty. "I think this..." Genie

caressed his engorged shaft, "...tells me that it's a lot." She giggled, but that faded away as he leaned in toward her. "Do you have any idea what this means to me?" She whispered against his lips, and the nerves in his belly jumbled and turned.

"If it's the same as what it means to me, then yes."

Their lips touched, hungrily mating as hands roamed and firmed, bodies mashed together uncaring as the water cooled around them.

His mouth left hers, and she arched over his arm, shivering slightly, just enough to break the sensual web. "Let's get out of here."

Genies' body was alive, burning with the need for his touch, while her knees threatened to give and her mind whirled with a sensual fog enveloping her.

Her breasts ached for his touch, and her core ... well, damn, it needed him to fill the emptiness—and not with fingers this time. No, she needed him. All of him. Right now.

She panted. "David?"

He lifted her, and she hung on, the abrasion of breasts to chest sending flickering flames through her body.

A moan escaped, and he laughed.

"The bedroom. We'll do this right."

She nodded, now mute as she stared at the visage before her, his face, tight with need, lips compressed and his eyes deep pools of green. She gulped as the emotions of the moment clogged her throat.

"I need..." The words lodged, but she needed to tell him how she felt, the primal urge forcing her to speak. Genie gasped as he tightened his arms around her, stopping still in the doorway to her—their—bedroom. "I ... I love you."

David's eyes closed, and for a moment her heart squeezed.

Oh God! He doesn't love me!

The thought ricocheted, but then he opened his eyes and a smile stole her breath.

"Thank God. Because I love you, too." He swooped in, and the urgency of before melted away as he kissed her softly and she slipped down his body, to stand on shaking feet.

The touch was an unspoken vow that coursed through her, filled her with warmth.

Now the movements were slow and unhurried. The air filled with soft cries as he caressed her damp wet skin, and she shuddered.

"I need you, Genie." His lips traced a fiery path down her throat to the sensitive spot at her collarbone. His tongue flicked lightly, and she groaned, cupping her hand to the back of his head, luxuriating in his silken hair.

His hand kneaded her breast lightly, thumb grazing over the distended bud of her nipple, and she whimpered while the pleasure pain reverberated.

"I'm going to make you scream tonight." His darkly erotic murmur held the promise of pleasure to come and her knees buckled. David carried her with swift strides to the coverlet and laid her down.

She stared, letting her body memorize the dips and planes of his body. A bead of water slipped down his chest to his abdomen, and she watched it disappear into the thatch of hair at his groin.

Dark and springy.

Genie reached a shaking hand toward him, touched the

flesh and heard his hiss as his cock jerked below her tender caress.

Even as she watched, moisture gathered at the slit, and unable to restrain herself she leaned in, swiped her tongue over it, delighting in the salty taste. Then her mouth opened over him, and he groaned, cupped her head, and guided her to take more.

"Oh God! You do that so well."

His words little more than an anguished whisper, and she increased the pace of her movements, his hips undulating slightly against her mouth, but he pulled away after only a few minutes of pleasure her body tingling with sensation and carnal hunger.

"Stop. Not like this."

Empty. Her body was empty and yearned for his intimate invasion. To be filled only by him. "Then come to me." Her hoarse demand propelled him forward, and he climbed onto the bed, spreading her legs until she was open to his view. Fire burned, and she could feel the dampness between her legs as desire pooled within her belly.

"Beautiful, so very beautiful."

Genie craved him. "Touch me, David. Feel how much I need you."

His fingers brushed her inner thighs, and the muscles clenched involuntarily as sensitive tissues cried out for release.

"Not yet. I want to savor this. Savor you."

"No. Come now."

David stayed still, closing his eyes as if re-gathering his strength. The very hunger rode her madly, the urge to mate primal. "Condom..." He dragged in a breath. "Where are the condoms?" He muttered and made to rise.

Genie stayed him, sitting up a little and placing a hand

on his leg. "There's some in my drawer. I bought them today."

He smiled. It was a hungry smile, that of a predator, and she gloried, because this was her predator.

Her lover. The man who loved her.

She snatched open the drawer, pulled out the unopened box, tugging at the security seal with shaking hands and fumbled. Swore fluently, then a strip of foil packs cascaded out, the cardboard tearing. "Damn." She tugged one off and pulled at the packaging. It didn't open. "Come on!" she whispered, hunger and desire ratcheting as air licked at her body, nipples budding even more tightly as they turned to pleasure-pain points.

He put his hands over hers, released her death grip. "Let me." One sure, quick move opened the foil pack, and he palmed the condom, his eyes never straying from hers. His hand moved to his groin, covering himself then grasping the rubber and rolling it down in a slow, sensual glide that ripped the breath from her body.

A groan filled the air, his or hers, she didn't care.

She needed him, damn it.

Now!

Genie pulled herself up, pushing at his shoulder so he fell backwards, the surprise on his face quickly replaced by a wolfish smile as the knowledge of what she was about to do descended.

She moved forward, over him until the tip of his erection touched the entry to her core. She gasped. The sensation was electrifying.

His hands rose, covered one breast, and held her hip on the other side as she gently, so very gently, impaled herself upon him.

David moved slowly as she sank down

He filled her.

Completely.

She gasped at the feel of him the sensation of fullness and her body urged her to move. Genie gave a tiny nudge and he clamped his hands at her waist, digging tight. Holding her still. She moaned, desperate for the heat and satisfaction.

"Don't. Move. Yet," he hissed, and she glanced at him, his eyes closed and jaw clenched, his chest heaving.

"David?"

"Just a minute. I need..." He sucked in a deep breath. "Now, Genie."

A nudge. The slightest of movements as she moved her hips, and she felt...dammit...she needed more.

Her body demanded the satisfaction it'd been denied for weeks and she undulated, moving faster and harder with each pass.

Deeper into the morass, she plunged with him, holding on tight as they pushed onwards, tightening the spring that coiled deep within her.

Fingernails bit into skin, broken murmurs and slapping flesh and the scent of musk and sex rose in the air.

"I need you, David. Please!" She heaved yet each time the peak rose, slowed her, his hands stilling her movements until madness and hunger was all that remained.

Their bodies damp from their joint shower and exertions slipped and slid against each other, heightening the senses as they moved.

She moaned again, as he rolled her over.

"I love you, David!" Genie cried the words, feeling him crush her breasts with his chest before his mouth devoured hers.

His lips moved over hers, tongues dancing against the other, and she lost herself in the dizzying taste of him.

Her fingers roamed his back while he pushed against her, rocking in the cradle of her thighs.

"Mine. You're mine now."

His hoarse voice left her shivering with desire.

"Always yours."

Leaning back, his hands ran down her body, tweaking her nipples until tiny arcs of pain erupted. David soothed them with gentle moves, and she writhed and thrust, yearned and finally arched up, her body releasing the pent-up pressures with a scream.

"David!"

He pumped faster and harder than before, eyes closed and head flung back, skin glistening with sweat before he finally stilled and her body milked him.

Then he slumped forward across her. "Mine.

Her eyes fluttered closed.

CHAPTER 9

David watched her sleep as nerves gnawed on his gut.

Should I ask her? Will she agree?

His stomach jittered and he carefully detangled himself from her body and headed for the bathroom to dispose of the condom. He'd rather not use one, would have preferred the feel of her body around him. But for now, until they'd settled, it took one more pressure off their budding relationship. David was determined that this time, this would last.

He loved her, and she loved him, but it was still so new.

Once cleaned up, he found his bag where he'd dropped it in the hallway, and hunted through it for the small package hidden within.

The one he'd bought last week.

The small velvet box didn't weigh much, but it carried his whole heart.

He released a ragged sigh and turned back to the doorway, spying her there, watching him in silence.

"Genie..." Suddenly every trace of surety was gone.

God, I want to ask her, but how?

"David?" Genie smiled shyly, and his answer was there. In his mind.

Just ask.

He hadn't planned anything, but he doubted it would've included getting down on one knee naked. David grinned. Just about everything between them though was out of the ordinary, so why not this?

He knelt.

Her face flamed, but she smiled. Her eyes shone.

"I know it's only been five weeks. But you know everything there is to know about me. You know my history. You know where I've fallen. I'm not perfect..." He stopped, watching a single tear trace its way down her beloved face. His stomach ached, but he continued on. "But I love you. I want us to be together. Forever."

Her shaking hand rose to her chest.

"Please. Say you'll marry me. Make an honest man of me and be around until we get too old to have sex."

Genie snorted. "Yeah. Like we'll ever be too old for that." She dropped to her knees in front of him. "You better stay with me forever. I don't know that I could cope if you weren't around. So yes. My answer is *yes*."

He held out the ring box.

"You're supposed to open it and put it on me. Not the other way around." She laughed, and he joined in, his shaking fingers fumbled on the catch. But when it opened she gasped.

"You said green was your favorite color." David pulled the intricately set emerald and diamond ring from its bed, and she extended her hand. The ring slipped on with ease. "This is a promise. One of love and eternity." He leaned in, carefully folded his arms around her and kissed her, sealing the vow.

THIS TIME AS THEY WAITED FOR HIS FRIENDS, GENIE knew what their reaction would be. She prepared herself. They wouldn't be happy, but this wasn't about them.

It was about her and David.

She sipped at her coffee waiting for the couples. "You know they're going to be surprised, don't you?"

"Yeah. I love you, and you love me. I don't want to waste a second of our lives. I want us to be together."

A warm feeling bloomed deep inside her.

"So how long...?" She broke off, because Karin and Michael made their way through the door, their daughter, Jemma cradled by the large man. She smiled; he was so careful with the newborn.

Behind them were Martine and Gordon, hand in hand.

Karin parked the pram beside the table and took a seat. "Hi. We thought we'd bring Jemma along for the outing. I couldn't bear to leave her with a sitter just yet."

Michael bent and brushed his lips over her cheek. "Hiya, Gene."

She kept her hand beneath the table, waiting until everyone was settled.

Then David cleared his throat. "We asked you all to come today, because we have an announcement."

All eyes focused on David and then her.

Genie wanted to squirm but didn't give in

This was their turn.

"I've asked Genie to marry me, and she's accepted."

Four shocked faces swiveled in her direction, but David wasn't finished yet.

"We know of, and appreciate your concern. Truly, we understand you're worried one or the other of us will be hurt. But life isn't about hiding from temptation or fate. If that's the way I'm supposed to live life, then it isn't worth living. But with Genie, I've discovered I can be who I'm meant to be. She doesn't give a rat's ass that I can't join her in having a drink of wine at night. She doesn't give a fig that I can't drive. She wants to be with me. That's the thing that counts."

Michael leaned forward. "It's all well and good to tell us you love each other, but you still have things…"

"We do, Michael, you're right." Genie extended her hand sporting the emerald ring and placed it on his. "But while it may be more than you had with Karin, we are committed to doing everything. I'm going to attend Partners AA, so I can understand and help. David and I have talked a lot. Everyone starts with a clean slate, and so, too, should David. I'm his, and he's mine. To us, that's what matters." She sat back, watching Michael's face, looking for a hint that he understood and accepted their decision.

"I promise you, Michael, that I have no intention of hurting Genie. And you know what? With her I feel whole. For the first time since…well, in my whole life. Karin? Do you understand?"

Three of the four weren't totally convinced, she could see it in their gazes and the way their mouths set. But they were David's closest friends. His greatest supporters, apart from her.

"This is *our* life. We appreciate your care and concern, but at the end of it, this is about *us*. We aren't going to do something to jeopardize what we have. Please. Trust us to make the right decisions." She waited for their reactions.

Gordon, Martine, and Michael nodded slowly as if accepting her words. It would be a long road, but the knot in her chest loosened just a little bit.

She watched Karin's smile grow. "I understand, probably more than anyone else here. I'm so pleased, David. Welcome to our crazy mixed up family, Genie."

Genie looked to Gordon and Martine, a lightness finally stealing the weight that'd been holding her down. They weren't fully convinced, but she detected a thawing in their attitude toward her. Maybe in time they'd accept what would be.

Gordon extended his hand. "If you're sure, then we'll support you. All the way. We've only ever wanted what was best for you."

Martine nodded, and the tight lump in Genie's chest released a little more.

She'd expected worse, so this positive turn was welcome.

They'd been there through the worst of David's struggles. They were like this because they cared.

"So, when do you plan…?" Karin nodded to her hand.

"Uh, we're thinking about seven months from now. My family's already making plans to come home. David's parents have also cleared time for the wedding."

"You will come, won't you?" She could detect the tension in his body as he addressed the four of them.

"We wouldn't miss it, would we?" Karin beamed. "Now, while on the subject of good news, how would you all like to be Jemma's godparents?"

Genie let loose the breath she was holding onto.

It was going to be okay.

CHAPTER 10

Their wedding day dawned clear and cool.

Genie woke in her bedroom. Her parents had requested she come home, but she couldn't. *This* was the place that was home to her now.

Instead, her sister and mother had come to stay the night.

David had stayed with Michael and Karin.

She grinned. It was just one more unusual aspect of their relationship. How many grooms stayed the night before their wedding at the house of their ex-partner? But of course, that made most sense, since he'd given up his apartment several weeks ago.

A small breeze, redolent with vanilla and chocolate teased her hair. "Yeah, okay. I know it's time for me to get up." She smiled. She'd taken to chatting to herself every time she felt and smelt that tiny puff, fancifully imagining it to be the spirit of young Emma Rose letting them know she was happy with the way things had worked out.

Genie headed to the bathroom and showered quickly,

using the vanilla and chocolate body wash she'd been unable to pass up.

Today she was marrying the man—maybe not a perfect one—but certainly the one from her fantasies.

Once she'd toweled dry, she headed for the bedroom to dress. Her sister, Zeta, would do her makeup and hair, and they would travel together in the small car to the church down the way. Neither Genie nor David wanted pomp and ceremony. The guest list was small, family and very close friends.

Her gown was simple, a three quarter length cream dress, which had been worn by her mother at her own wedding. David's mother had provided the headpiece she'd worn at hers.

A knock on the door surprised her. "Come in."

Her mother entered, looking teary. "So the day has finally dawned. My little girl is getting married."

"Yes, Mum. It's here." She grinned at the reflection in the mirror.

Zeta crowded into the bedroom with her torture instruments— hairdryer and rollers—in hand. Not to mention a big metal box, full of cosmetics no doubt.

"Zeta, honey, it's so good to have you here as well." Her mother practically burst with pride.

"Well, you know, I've wanted to attack Genie's hair for a long time. How could I possibly turn down this once in a lifetime opportunity?"

She could hear the humor in her sister's voice.

"Are you ... are you sure? Is this what you want?" Her mother's words floated over her, and Genie smiled.

Her mother only wanted the best for her. But she knew, without a shadow of a doubt, this was the right choice.

"I've never been surer of anything in my life, Mum. I love him so much." Tears burned in her eyes.

"Then you're doing the right thing." Her mother dabbed at tears with her ever-present handkerchief.

From that point, the day became a whirl of activity as her hair was arranged and her makeup applied. The next thing she knew, it was down the steps and accepting a bouquet from Karin who met her at the door of the church with a tight hug.

"He's truly one of the best men I've ever met. I know you'll be happy together."

She breathed deeply, and for a moment, was sure she heard a child's laugh. All in her mind of course.

Then the doors opened, and she made her way down the aisle of the half full church.

Her vision narrowed until all she could see was David, where he waited for her, smiling and the peace and tranquility of him was a balm soothing her.

Genie placed her hand in his, and together they marched forward to make their vows.

His voice was strong and clear and hers trembling but sure, and *finally* the band of gold slipped over the knuckle of her hand, the weight reminding her of the gravity of their promises.

Michael and Karin were the first to congratulate them, and their mutual longtime friend hugged her close. "Congratulations, Genie. I'm so pleased you've found your other half."

Just as they stepped out of the church the playful breeze caught their attention as it caught up the leaves falling from the trees, and then letting them settle in little piles on the ground.

She smiled at David.

EPILOGUE

Several Months Later

"It's a damn good thing I didn't sign up for another period of enlistment, isn't it?" Genie patted her belly lightly before scrunching the paper bag containing the box and throwing it into the small bin.

She'd purposely waited until today to check, even though she'd been suspicious for several days.

Genie smiled catching sight of the two little pink lines on the white plastic testing device perched on the side of the bath. "Hmm, guess we'd better go tell Daddy then, shouldn't we?" She picked up the item when a stray breeze carrying a faint waft of chocolate and vanilla, riffled her hair. It felt like a ghostly kiss on the side of her cheek, and she raised a hand to the spot, then snorted. "My, what an imagination you have these days, Genie," she muttered as she headed to the door and swung it open, but the feeling of being watched remained as she headed down the hall to the kitchen.

Her husband of some months, David, had her made a

cup of tea daily for the last week, since her appetite had been precarious.

For the first few days she'd thought it had to be a stomach bug, but since then a suspicion had formed in her mind.

She'd been fairly sure, though, when she'd gone to the pharmacy. She'd had all the natural signs, sore breasts, and nausea in the morning, and coupled with no period in the last month.

They'd talked about babies. He'd told her how he loved them and when Genie was ready they could try. It seemed like there was no trying for them though, if this was an indication of their fertility. She giggled.

One last rub at her tummy, hoping to soothe the butterflies, she entered the kitchen.

"Hey. Feeling better now?" His green eyes crinkled with concern as his fingers swept over her cheek.

She nuzzled in, holding the secret close to herself for just a few more minutes. "Yeah. But you know what? You have a later start today, right? Let's go sit in the lounge and cuddle."

He eyed her, and she thought she detected a brief flash of concern in his gaze. A swift pat of her hand on his lightened his countenance slightly, and she fretted knowing how touchy he was about illness.

"It's nothing serious. Honestly."

David nodded and gave her a careful kiss.

Together they walked to the small front room and settled into their favored spots on the love seat they'd bought on their honeymoon.

"Okay, so I do have something to tell you. It's to do with my not feeling so flash for the last week or two."

He leaned forward making to say something, but she placed a soft finger against his lips.

"Just let me finish, okay?"

David watched her, and Genie paused. What was the best way to tell him the good news?

"All right."

"So, I've been feeling unwell. Yesterday I went to the pharmacy and bought a home testing kit." She reached out with her other hand and laid the plastic item in his waiting hands. "Surprise. It's positive."

He stilled, looking at her then glancing down. Inch by inch a smile crept over his face. "Positive?"

She nodded as hot tears formed.

"Today was her birthday. What a gift you've given me." David's voice went husky.

As he opened his arms, the breeze blew one last time through the open window, riffling her hair then his as he pulled her against him.

"Thank you, Genie. For everything. But especially for this. This day is now doubly special to me." He reached out, tugged her into his embrace and kissed her.

His caress was light. His fingers touched her cheek softly, and Genie sighed, twisting so she could move in closer. The warmth of his body scorched her, but she craved his heat, yearned for his caresses and kisses.

Their tongues tangled intimately, and his hand slid down from her shoulder, brushing the straps to the side, leaving her top gaping slightly.

He pulled away, glassy eyed as he surveyed the way she sprawled in his arms.

Every inch of her body tingled, and need speared through her.

"Oh, Genie, do you have any idea how much I love you?"

Her breath hitched. "I hope so."

David slipped the other strap down so the top dipped slightly, catching on her sensitive breasts.

She hissed, and he smiled, while her belly turned to mush. With care, he brushed his hands over her collarbone, and she squirmed beneath his fiery touches, whimpering for more as her body readied itself for him.

Her breath caught as his hands skated over her sensitive nipples, then bucked as one hand found its way to the apex of her thighs, kneading slightly.

He bunched the light skirt up, seeking the damp hot folds that lay below as he carefully pushed her panties askew. His fingers grazed her core slightly, and she stiffened in his arms.

Genie tugged at his shirt with shaking fingers, need coursing through her.

He pulled away long enough for her to rid him of the material, and she laid her palms flat against his smooth hard flesh, hissing again at the electric feel of him. His hands moved swiftly to tug the skirt and panties from her, and she lifted up.

Moving quickly, she wriggled off his lap before she allowed him to lift her small top away. Then she was bare beneath his molten gaze. "Oh, David, you're still over-dressed! Take it off." Her chest heaved as her body ignited beneath his knowing touch.

Her husband grinned like a rakish pirate and cocked his head to one side. "Madam wants me naked? Then madam shall have what she wants." David's hands dropped to the button and zip closure, slowly teasing her as she watched him shuck his clothes until he, too, was naked in the dappled sunlight, his skin flushed with need and his erection now freed from its confines.

He stepped forward, and she put out a shaking hand. The glorious satiny feel of his cock warm and vibrant beneath her touch nearly stole her senses. He led her to the bedroom, slowly pushing her down to their bed then he followed. Smoky eyes told of his need, along with the seeping fluid at the end of his erection.

She made to grip it, but he moved away.

"Not yet. Not that way." The huskiness of his voice left her shuddering with anticipation.

David covered her, one hand already testing her readiness while she moaned. Clever lips found the tip of her breast, tongue flicking as fire streaked.

She bucked against his fingers, riding them slightly. Her heart raced, and her hands gripped his shoulders, looking for an anchor in the wild sea of sensation.

His mouth moved to her other nipple, and she bowed off the bed. Hot. She was so hot and needy. Emptiness clawed at her, deep inside. Only he could love her the way she needed right now.

"No more. I want you inside me!" Genie pushed up, and he raised his head, smiling before leaning back toward her for a fiery kiss.

His mouth working over her while she tasted his essence. His hands moved to her thighs, making space as he positioned himself, and then with a single glide, he slid within.

Her body welcomed him, gripped at his long length. She pulled her mouth away, sucking in air as he moved. She met his undulating thrusts with needy cries and jerky motions.

The movements were slow and sensuous. His hands

roamed over her body, fondling and firming everywhere they went.

"Oooh! Yes, David. More!" Her fingers tangled in his hair, and the pace swept her along on a tide of passion, each move tightening the pressure which formed deep in her belly.

Suddenly the peak crested, and Genie's orgasm crashed through her, the same instant it took David, too. He stilled, holding himself deep within her. Then slowly he lowered them to the bed. The racing of his heart was evident beneath her languid hand, which still lay against his chest.

"I love you," Genie whispered and he clutched her tightly to him.

"And I love you, too. And the life we are making together." David kissed the top of her head, and she smiled.

The End

In the darkness evil waits…

As a young bride Kira was whisked away from every
thing and everyone she knew, including her new husband
and became Christina, an operative of the Displaced
Persons Unit.

As the danger grows she sees an opportunity to save her
husband Vasya and sister Serina. But nothing is the same.
Serina is grown up—married and pregnant.

Vasya too is older and darkly forbidding. Trusting Christina doesn't come easily until a catastrophic event takes place. Now, knowing the truth everything he thought he knew is changed. But at a very high cost.

The four must work together to defeat the Demon, Zuor and the stakes are higher than they imagined and all could be lost.

The burning at the back of her neck warned she was being watched. A quick glance didn't clarify it. Instead, she turned around in time to see her mother's face, pale. "Mama?"

She took a step forward, but her grandfather snatched her wrist.

The grip was painful, and Kira stilled. "Let your parents talk."

She didn't know what the topic of conversation was, but it couldn't be good.

The dappled sunlight seemed cooler than before.

Her father crooked his forefinger at her grandfather while they stood there. For a moment she wished Vasya had come with them, but he had to work. Just the thought of her new husband warmed Kira.

She only had a few minutes to contemplate her newly defined status as a married woman, when her grandfather pulled at her hand. "Come with me." He tugged and, confused, Kira allowed herself to be towed away.

A glance at her parents' faces stole any feeling of well-being.

"Grandfather?"

"Shh, my love. You must go." His grip was implacable and his face stern, but he shivered.

"What are you doing? Where are you taking me, Grandfather?"

They moved rapidly through the village they'd visited to sell their wares just that morning, and for the first time since they'd arrived in the market place she felt fear. What was wrong? Was it something to do with Vasya?

"You are in danger. We must send you away." The words confused her further. Send her away? Danger?

"Where is Vasya?" She stumbled over a stone, but he kept tugging her onwards.

With a quick glance around, he hauled her into a dirty laneway between the buildings. Kira gasped, trying to drag air into her starving lungs. "There's no time. We must get you away."

A nondescript shopfront lay ahead, and he pushed on the door. It rattled and opened with a loud groan. "Andre? Andre, are you here?"

An older man shuffled into the room, bent nearly double from the weight of the load on his back. "Marat? What do you want?"

"My granddaughter. They are coming for her and us. Get her away. Take her now, while you can."

The man's face clouded over. "Are you sure?"

"Grandfather, where is Vasya?" Fright had the blood in her veins pounding.

"Hush, my precious. Andre will see you well." He turned. "Whatever it takes, Andre. Take her now." With surprising speed, her grandfather whirled and was gone.

The man, Andre, eyed her. "Come this way, child. There is no time to be lost."

Eleven years later

The tattoo of her heart and cry of terror woke her, as they usually did. Once again, as she had since that rapid flight from those who sought her, she found herself in a lonely bed. Hundreds of miles away from everything she'd dreamed of, in a house she'd built for them to share. As always, it left her wishing that Vasya had fled with her.

Instead, here she was, exiled without her husband. With a sob, she rolled over and let the tears fall.

Available from Beachwalk Press
books2read.com/IOTB

Direct Autographed Copy
http://bit.ly/2w6g4K6

When Cupid—otherwise known as Diocail— is banished from his home on a remote Scottish Island, he's set a series of tasks by the great god Lugh, who also happens to be his father.

In **Blame The Wine**, he must bring two lovers together... BBW Cara and James, the man she's lusted over from afar who happens to be a super geek and head Veha Industries.

In **A Stranger's Embrace**, Diocail is driven to help

an emotionally fragile Jane and Davis, a famous author. The task is more complicated, with the existence of Carstairs her could-be ex-husband and teenage daughter, Frannie.

In **_Revenge on Cupid_**, Diocail must take the ultimate chance and find his own happily ever after with Simone. Sometimes the past gets in the way and HEA's don't come cheap though.

The dusty, dingy little diner was full, even with its current state of cleanliness—or lack thereof. People from the surrounding offices didn't care about anything except the incredible, well-prepared food at a reasonable cost. They flooded in, like waves to the shore. As one tide left, another swept in.

"Honestly, Simone. I'm going to try getting his attention one more time. If that doesn't work, I'm out of there. I mean, how long can I keep trying?" Cara picked at the caramel tart she hadn't been able to resist with the cheap metal fork and flicked the blob of fresh cream that sat on top to the side of the plate.

"You've said that tons of times before. Besides, what are you going to do to get his attention? Hmm? Walk naked through the typing pool?" Simone bobbed the straw in her smoothie as she eyed her friend with a frown. "It's been what? Eighteen months since you saw him, and you've mooned over him from a distance ever since you met him. You need to move on, Cara. That is, unless there's something you haven't shared?"

The query was arch. Cara shivered even as she shook her head. "No."

Simone quirked an eyebrow, obviously unconvinced with the answer. Cara let out a deep sigh of frustration. "There's a position...it's only temporary, for a PA reporting directly to him." She speared a forkful of tart, chewed quickly and swallowed, before continuing. "In his office, full-time for the period of the engagement. I saw the memo yesterday. I mean, I have the skills, right? I can type, answer phones, make coffee, file, greet people. What's more, I can probably do it better than all those size eights in the typing pool that Ms. Jackman seems to prefer." She nodded thoughtfully. "All I have to do is get past the ogre in Human Resources."

Simone stared at her, disbelief clear on her face. "Girl, I so remember that woman. If you think you can get past her, you're doing better than I ever did. That's why I left Veha Industries, remember? Maybe it's time to haul out your resumé and consider some other options. Look for something better." Simone shook her head and billows of her crimson hair swirled through the still air.

Cara understood Simone only had her best interests at heart. But this time she knew the outcome would be different. Hell, she could feel it in the air. The tingle of expectation.

"Cara, the HR ogre will hang you out for breakfast before she offers you anything like a position in that office. Remember her mantra? Good looks and good work make for a positive workplace!"

Simone didn't sugar-coat anything. It was another great reason for their long- term friendship. Honesty. But Cara didn't want to hear the truth in the statement. Even if it was exactly as her friend said.

Cara nodded quickly. "Yeah, I know, but if I don't try, then I won't know how close I can get to him, right? And the only way to catch his attention is to get past *her* and see him in person." Cara quaked a little at the information she needed to share. The favor she needed to ask. "Anyway, I tidied up my resumé and dropped the application into a memo envelope yesterday, so it's too late to back out now. I mean, fortune favors the brave. Doesn't it? If I don't snag an interview, I'm going to visit the career advisor across the street and register with them." She shrugged. "I'll look for temp work until something more long-term shows up. I can see what they have on offer and well...who knows? Maybe a job with the right boss is just waiting for me. But I'd rather this worked out, to be honest." Her voice trailed off into a whisper. "I really wish he would notice me."

Simone took a long slurp of her banana drink, and Cara noticed her questioning gaze even as she squirmed. Finally, Simone nodded. "It's your funeral. So anyway, you'd better show me this memo if you want me to be a referee for you. I'm guessing that's what you need, right? I'll have to know what I'm supposed to say about you before they ring."

Cara smiled. "Thanks, Simone. I knew I could count on you." She slipped a piece of paper out of her handbag and handed it over. "Sorry it's a bit creased. It was in the bottom of my bag, I stashed it so none of the others from the pool would see. You know how it is."

Available from Love Books Publishing
books2read.com/CelticCupid

Direct Autographed Copy
http://bit.ly/2vs7wtS

Can a cyber-enhanced warrior and a ship's captain find love together?

Levia Endrado never wanted to be a warrior, but at seventeen she was deemed suitable for battle. After intense training and multiple enhancements, which gave her superior strength and healing ability, she was sent off to defeat the enemy—a killing machine with a mission.

When the war was over, she had to find a new life. At twenty-seven she's a washed-up veteran without a future. Or she was, until she met Sandon Daria.

Serving as a pilot aboard Sandon's spaceship the *Golden Echo* makes Levia long for a different and gentler life. But old hurts and even older enemies aren't so easily forgotten. Particularly when they come back for her.

Sandon is determined to show Levia that she's more than just a BioCybe...she's the woman who completes him. Getting close is just the first step, keeping her alive is an even bigger challenge, but one he's willing to take because the prize is their combined future.

Levia scanned the long line of other hopefuls entering the chamber. The large building in the center of town was cold, and she dragged her wrap around her body, even as she craned her head, looking to the high ceiling. She'd never before had an occasion to enter the testing complex, yet she'd seen the lines of teenagers every time they passed the building.

Once she'd asked her parents why the teens were lined up and her mother's face had shuttered. Her stepfather had just shaken his head and growled. They'd stopped her questions with a carefully uttered, "You'll know soon enough, Levia." The pain in her mother's eyes had been enough to shush her questions. For endless months afterward, her parents had traveled different routes to the educational facility she attended and Levia lost interest in the puzzle of that building.

Now, as she looked around, remembering that long ago spring day, it was her opportunity to find out. But she felt a surge of concern at what lay ahead. She likely wasn't the only one, given that there were probably two to three hundred seventeen-year-olds gathered in the one place. Ahead of her, she caught sight of a couple of girls, their arms linked together and wide smiles on their faces. Scanning the crowd, she became aware that, by far, a majority of those gathered displayed both fear and trepidation.

"All female subjects will enter through doors three, six, and seven. All male subjects will enter through gates four, eight, and ten." The speaker above her was loud, and she jumped before checking the numbers etched on the black metal sign over her head.

The massive doors beside her swung open, and now an uncertain silence reigned. Many of the youngsters hung back, clearly discomforted by whatever testing regime lay ahead. This was where they'd been told their futures would be determined.

"Oh gosh, I hope they only have an aptitude and psych eval. I don't think..." Levia turned to see the white face of the girl behind her. The girl had uttered what many must silently be thinking.

Levia dragged an unsteady breath in, her hand resting flat against the plane of her belly as she looked around. No one had entered yet. It was clear many were on the verge of taking the step, but still they hung back.

She straightened her shoulders. "I'm not afraid." It was always wiser to approach things head-on, she believed. When her biological father had died, she'd been one of the few to view his capsule before it was sent into the massive gray structure built to accommodate those who'd moved onto the next life realm.

Her legs shook as she wobbled toward the entrance. Beyond the doorway, she spied sealed cubicles and her heart stuttered. Why cubicles? Usually testing—med and psych—were in eval-units, hidden only by billowing white curtains. She glanced back, noting that others had taken the first step.

"Move along, subjects." Once again, the androgynous voice of the address system blared.

Of course, given it was her seventeenth anniversary of birth, she was technically considered an adult now.

She thought longingly of baby Rald and her half-sister, Elda, waiting at home for her to return, and the celebrations to be held that night. That made her smile. She would need to make them proud of her.

She entered a row and the tall Educational Specialist, the edu-specs as her peers laughingly called them, stopped her. "Present your credentials to the scanner."

She'd done this many times since the tiny implant had been slipped below the dermal layer of her skin at birth. The small unit in her wrist heated as her details were checked.

"Enter the first cubicle, Levia Endrado, and follow the instructions to complete your assessment."

Thus dismissed, Levia moved to the first unit, laid her palm against the scanner, and the door slid open soundlessly.

"Welcome, Levia Endrado. Take your place in the eval-unit." The soft contralto of the voice echoed after the door closed silently behind her.

"What are you evaluating?" Her voice was breathy, and she peered around.

"Your   skills—physical   and   psychological.   Your

emotional and medical status. Your educational attainment levels."

It was an answer that shed little insight into the many things she was hungry to know. "Why do all seventeen year olds—"

"Take a seat, Levia. Then we may begin your testing."

If she'd expected an answer, she was sadly mistaken, she considered sourly. She dropped into the seat, the soft leather-like surface molding to her body.

"Levia Endrado, you are required to remove all non-specified apparel."

She jolted in the chair. "It's cold."

"The temperature will be amended. Remove the non-specified apparel."

Her misgivings grew as she dragged off the light wrap she'd brought with her, and then threw it to the floor at the side of the unit.

"We will begin, Levia Endrado. At any time, should you experience any malfunctions of the unit, simply depress the red button." It glowed and she grimaced.

Levia reclined against the chair and waited for the testing to begin.

The first examination was based on her understanding of the political system, where she saw herself, and her knowledge of the rights and responsibilities accorded through citizenship of both her planet and the commonwealth.

The second test was mathematical and scientific proficiency. It felt like hours had passed by the time she'd finished, and she lay limp on the seat, exhausted.

"Levia Endrado, you may rise. The sanitary unit will emerge once you trigger the yellow button at the door.

Should you require refreshment, press the blue button and a restorative will be made available."

"Can I leave?"

"Negative, Levia Endrado. Your needs will be catered for in this capsule."

"Why?" Her voice hitched and true fear rose for the first time. Why did they keep her in the alcove?

"All will be revealed at the end of the testing cycle."

Levia looked at the now empty screen before hurling a curse word. It was met with silence.

The urgent throb of her bladder reminded her that she needed to use the facilities, so, with

a sigh, she rose and clambered from the seat. After attending to the needs of her body, she walked around the unit, peering at the door, but it was obviously programmed remotely. She poked and prodded, but it made no difference. With a huff, she headed back to the chair.

The moment she'd settled in, the viewing screen shone bright. "Welcome back, Levia. The next sequence will evaluate your psychological reflexes, then that will be followed up with the general knowledge portion of the evaluation."

"When can I leave?" It seemed better to ask bluntly, she told herself.

"Once the examination is completed. After the next set of evaluations, you will be subjected to the physical aspect."

"Then I can go home?"

"Levia Endrado, you will now complete the psychological test. This will be undertaken by one of the center's personal evaluators."

She frowned. Personal evaluators? She bit her lip, and the sting reminded her that this wasn't something to joke about. In her seventeen years, she'd only heard of personal evaluators being brought in once before, and that was when one of the girls at her academy had been in a serious accident. Both legs were amputated and her body's ability to keep her alive had been gravely compromised. Her peers had been informed that the girl had requested the assessment before she could request her support systems be disconnected.

"Levia Endrado, are you ready to recommence processing?" The emotionless voice echoed once more and she gulped.

"Yes."

Available from Beachwalk Press
http://www.beachwalkpress.com

Direct Autographed Books
http://bit.ly/BioCybe

<u>Warriors of the Elector</u>

- Star of Ishtar
- Starline
- Starfire
- Star of the Fleet
- Starburst
- The Star of Eternity

The Star of Ishtar & Starline - Print

Starfire & Star of the Fleet - Print

Starburst & The Star of Eternity - Print

<u>Blood Secrets (Re-releasing 2020)</u>

- The Blood Bride
- The Illuminated Witch
- The Sorcerer's Touch

<u>The Search Duology</u>

- Miss Elspeth's Desire
- Miss Isabelle's Craving

<u>Reunion Trilogy</u>

- War's End
- The Assassin

- Executing Justice

The Reunion Trilogy in Paperback

Sex Love & Aliens

- Tangled Webs
- False Webs
- Covert Webs

21st Testing Protocol

- Cyborg: Redux
- Children Of A Greater Evil
- When Evil Came To Stay (Not Yet Released)
- Finis: The War To End All Wars (Not Yet Released)

Celtic Cupid Trilogy

- Blame The Wine
- A Stranger's Embrace
- Revenge On Cupid

The Celtic Cupid Trilogy in Paperback

Zombieology

- The Reset (2018)
- I Dream of Zombies (2019)
- The Six Million Dollar Zombie (Not Yet Released)

Knights of Pleasure

- Silken Knights (Not Yet Released)

Single Titles

The Chocolate Affair (also in Print)

Falling In Love Again (Previously A Sapphire For Karina)

BioCybe (also in Print)

Hesparia's Tears (also in Print)

Tomorrow's Promise

A Bar In Paris (also in Print)

Inheritance Of The Blood (also in Print)

The Plan

Loving Memories (also in Print)

Hero of Heartbreak Hill (also in Print)

Raspberry Dreams (Not Yet Released)

Non Fiction

Self Publishing: Absolute Beginners Guide (With Suzi Love)

Written as Ciara Cave

25 Curated Ways To Get Rid Of Telemarketers

Book Signings for Absolute Beginners

ABOUT THE AUTHOR

Imogene is published in a range of romance genres including Paranormal, Science Fiction and Contemporary. She is mainly published in the UK and USA.

In 2010, Imogene Nix (the pen name not Imogene herself) was born. Imogene sat down and worked tirelessly for 3 months culminating in the book Starline, which became the first in a trilogy titled, "Warriors of the Elector." Since then she's had over 30 titles published and is now focusing on hybridising herself - with a mixture of traditionally published and self-published works.

In fact, she's taking control of many of her back catalogue books, which are slowly re-releasing as self-published titles.

Imogene is a member of a range of professional organisations world wide, and believes in the mantra of mentoring and paying it forward and is actively involved in mentorship (through NaNoWrimo and her vlog: In The Chair With Imogene Nix) and tutoring of new and upcoming authors.

In her spare time she loves to drink coffee, wine & eat chocolate and is parenting her spoiled dog and a ferocious cat along with her husband and 2 human daughters and looks forward to weekends away with her husband in their caravan "The Seven Year Hitch!" Do look forward to her caravan romance at some point!

To Contact Imogene
www.imogenenix.net
imogene@imogenenix.net

facebook.com/ImogeneNix

twitter.com/ImogeneNix

instagram.com/ImogeneNix

9 781922 369000